A Winning Edge

by
BONNIE BLAIR

with Greg Brown

Illustrations by Doug Keith

TAYLOR PUBLISHING
Dallas, Texas

Greg Brown lives in Bothell, Washington, with his wife Stacy and two children. His children's book with Troy Aikman, *Things Change*, was a national best-seller, as was his book with Cal Ripken Jr., *Count Me In*. Greg is also the co-author of *Be the Best You Can Be* with Kirby Puckett and *Patience Pays* with Edgar Martinez. Brown regularly speaks at schools and can be reached at his Internet address: PFKGB@AOL.COM

Doug Keith provided the illustrations for the best-selling children's books, *Things Change* with Troy Aikman, and *Count Me In* with Cal Ripken Jr. His illustrations have appeared in national magazines such as *Sports Illustrated for Kids*, greeting cards, and books.

Published by Taylor Publishing
      1550 West Mockingbird Lane
      Dallas, Texas 75235

Library of Congress Cataloging-in-Publication Data

Printed in the United States of America

10   9   8   7   6   5   4   3   2   1

Over the years Bonnie Blair has given back to the Champaign community that so generously supported her financial training needs during her skating career. Bonnie gives of her time and money to a number of organizations, including the Champaign police department, which organized fund-raisers for her. Money raised by the annual Bonnie Blair Golf Tournament now is donated to the American Brain Tumor Association.

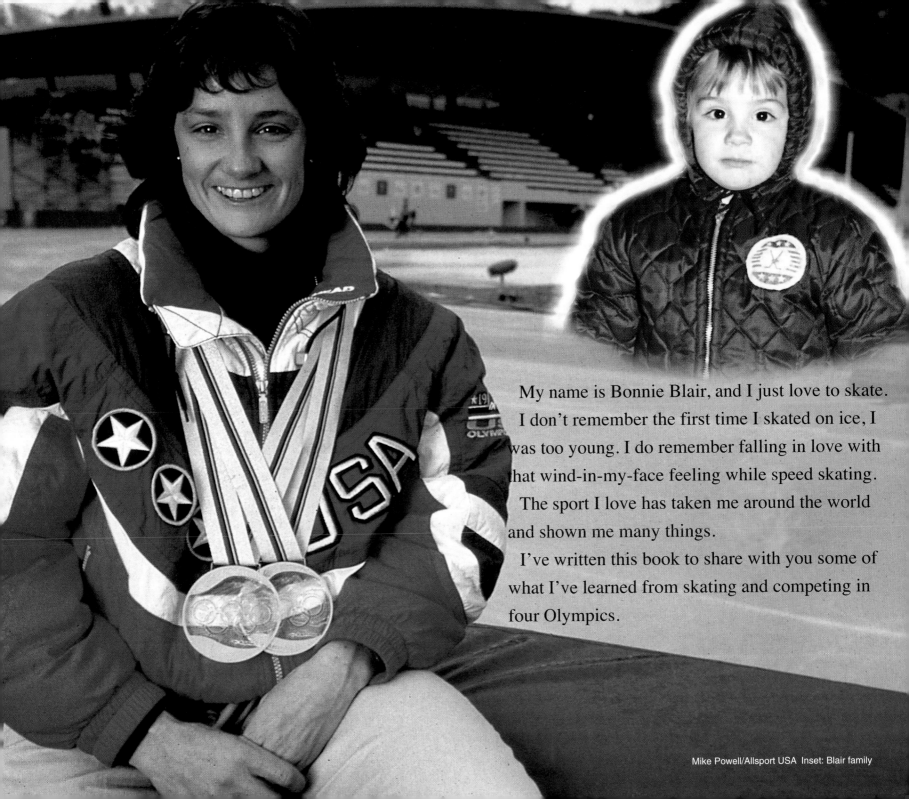

My name is Bonnie Blair, and I just love to skate. I don't remember the first time I skated on ice, I was too young. I do remember falling in love with that wind-in-my-face feeling while speed skating.

The sport I love has taken me around the world and shown me many things.

I've written this book to share with you some of what I've learned from skating and competing in four Olympics.

Mark Baker/Reuter

I look back sometimes and can't believe all that's happened to me thanks to skating.

Speed skating has taken me farther than I ever dreamed possible.

Bonnie's Highlights

- The first American female to win five gold medals in Olympic history.
- The most decorated U.S. athlete in the Winter Olympics.
- First American to win a gold medal in the same Winter event in three Olympic Games.
- 11 gold medals at World Sprint Championships
- 10-time U.S. National Sprint Champion, 1985–1994

Olympic Medals

- Gold medal, 500 meters, 39.25 seconds, Lillehammer, Norway, 1994
- Gold medal, 1,000 meters, 1:18.74 seconds, Lillehammer, Norway, 1994
- Gold medal, 500 meters, 40.33 seconds, Albertville, France, 1992
- Gold medal, 1,000 meters, 1:21.90 seconds, Albertville, France, 1992
- Gold medal, 500 meters, 39.10 seconds, Calgary, Canada, 1988
- Bronze medal, 1,000 meters, 1:18.31 seconds, Calgary, Canada, 1988

World Records

- 500 meters, 38.69, February 1995
- 500 meters, 38.99, March 1994
- 500 meters, 39.10, Calgary Olympics, 1988
- World Sprint Speed Skating Championship overall points, 1994
- World Sprint Speed Skating Championship overall points, April 1992
- World Sprint Speed Skating Championship overall points, Jan. 1992
- World Sprint Speed Skating Championship overall points, April 1989

Shaun Botterill/Allsport USA

Now that I'm retired from speed skating, one of the things I enjoy is talking to people all over the country.

I share with them four key words that helped make my dreams come true. They are: dedication, balance, risk and love.

AP photo

Skating in the Olympics, with the whole world watching, was special, whether I won or not. But most of my races have not been on TV. In fact, only a few hundred people saw one of my most memorable races. It came toward the end of my career in Calgary, Canada. One March day in 1994, I edged to the start line with my eyes set on breaking the world record in the 500-meter race. No woman had ever skated that distance faster than 39 seconds. I tried many years and always came up short.

This race wasn't about gold medals, fame or money. It was about racing against myself. I brought calm confidence to the start line, like always. Power bolted through my legs as choppy steps brought me up to maximum speed. I felt in the groove before the first turn. The rush of the wind against my face put me back, for a moment, to a frozen pond and the pure joy of gliding on ice.

Blair family

I've skated ever since I can remember. I loved the freedom to turn any direction I pleased. I remember the thrill of going fast, but most of all I remember wanting to skate every day.

Blair family

Blair family

I'm told I stood on skates before I could walk.
My parents slipped skates over my baby shoes so I
could be on the ice with my brothers and sisters.

On the day of my birth, my dad dropped Mom
off at a hospital and took the rest of the family to a
skating race.

They heard about my birth when the rink
announcer said: "Looks like Charlie's family has
just added another skater."

Born the youngest of six kids, skating seemed
natural to me. I watched my siblings skate in
hundreds of races as I grew up.

Blair family

Blair Family

Blair Family

Blair Family

During the winter, our weekends revolved around races. I just loved skating around the track, waving and pretending to race. My parents didn't push me into skating. They simply introduced me. We became instant friends, speed skating and me.

I grew up in Champaign, Illinois, about 135 miles south of Chicago. We would drive hours on the weekends to compete. I started racing when I was four. Back then, we raced short-track, which means a group of skaters raced against each other at the same time. I don't remember the first race I won. I do remember the first time I tasted victory, I wanted more. Winning was common in our family. My brothers and sisters were state and national champions.

Early on, I learned from them that winning takes dedication. As you can see in this picture, we often woke early to practice. I didn't mind. Knowing I would skate that day made me smile, even at six in the morning.

Blair Family

Being just a kid, I often could not last a whole day at the rink watching races and competing. Most meets I fell asleep on Mom's lap with my special blanket. I sometimes even slept through my races. I could fall asleep anywhere with my "blankey." My parents let me sleep through my races to show me winning and losing when you are young really does not matter.

Believe it or not, I still have that blanket, although if I washed it one more time it would probably fall apart. I slept with my blankey under my pillow all the way through junior high.

Many of our races were outdoors. I remember traveling to Chicago when I was ten for a state championship race. The second day, the temperature dropped and the wind howled, making the windchill 80 degrees below zero.

The cold stung like needles on my face and the wind sliced through my clothes. I had no desire to race. I felt worried because we drove a long way and rented a motel room. I didn't want to let my parents down. I thought they'd say, "We've spent all this money, driven all this way . . . you can't quit now."

Through chattering teeth I finally said: "Dad, I don't think I want to race. It's freezing out there."

"That's fine," he said.

That was that. We went home.

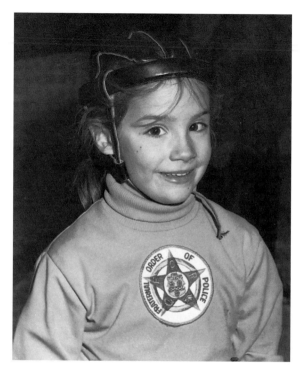

When we did race, Dad always used to stand at the finish line with a stopwatch. I think he enjoyed timing our races as much as we loved racing. His best advice before a race was: "Get out in front and stay there."

If we had a bad race, he'd always say, "Well, we'll get 'em next time."

My parents didn't make a big deal about it if we won or lost. I guess that is what kept racing fun for me when I was young. I knew my parents loved me no matter how I raced. That helped keep me balanced.

Long before I ever won a race, my brothers and sisters had brought home hundreds of skating trophies. They were stored in our basement on rows of shelves. I remember taking friends downstairs and showing them our wall of gold. As I started winning, I put mine in a special place. But I never raced just for a trophy. Maybe seeing all those trophies collect dust downstairs made me realize there is more to winning than trophies and medals.

Blair Family

Blair Family

Reading the words on trophies proved tough for me at times. That's because I'm farsighted. I can see things far away fine, but things up close can be a little blurry.

In first grade, I started wearing glasses. As brothers and sisters sometimes do, mine teased me. They called me, "Polly Professor." I hated it. I worried about what people at school thought and probably didn't wear my glasses as often as I should have.

My family also teased me about playing the violin. In second grade, I decided I wanted to learn how to play the violin. My brothers and sisters used to cover their ears when I played at home. The screeching, scratching noise I made wasn't music to anyone's ears.

I tried for about a year but never could learn to play well. At our class recital, I had to watch everyone else to know when to move my bow up and down. My heart wasn't into it.

That's probably because the real reason I started was to stay out of the cold. During winter at our school, those in music stayed inside during recess to practice. This might sound odd, but deep down I didn't want to play out in the cold, so I tried the violin.

Some people might say that because I gave up the violin I quit. The way I look at it, I tried something new and it just didn't work out. One of the best parts of being a kid is trying different things to learn what interests you. Nobody is good at everything. We all have our own special tastes and talents. I tried lots of other sports besides skating. I was good at some, terrible at others.

I used to swim during the summer. Just before one season started, I had grown tired of swimming. I feared my parents would make me and worried about it for weeks. Finally, I told them, "I don't think I want to turn out for swimming." They said, "That's fine."

In high school, I earned B's and C's; I enjoyed math the most. I became a cheerleader, ran track, and played softball.

Some, like my brother Rob, teased me about how I throw a softball. Many girls throw just as well as boys. I, however, always have had an awkward throwing motion. I'm a good hitter, but I still haven't figured out how to throw well.

Even though I'm not the best softball player, I still have fun playing.

Blair Family

As I learned from swimming, there are times when sports are not fun. There are times to quit and times to keep trying. When I turned twelve I didn't have much fun skating and thought about quitting.

I had a tough year because I suddenly became clumsy on the ice as my body started changing.

People think that because I won Olympic medals I won every race I ever skated. That's just not true.

I fell all the time during races that season. Part of me wanted to quit and part of me was going crazy. My friends and family kept encouraging me to stick with skating. They said I would grow out of my awkwardness. They were right, and I finally started to improve again.

At the time, short-track racing was not an Olympic sport as it is today. I never dreamed about racing in the Olympics—until one day my dad planted a seed in my soul.

Some days I would ride my bike to visit my dad at his work as a city civil engineer. One day, he introduced me to a co-worker. He said, "This is my daughter Bonnie. Some day she's going to skate in the Olympics and win a medal."

"Yeah right, Dad," I thought to myself. "Short-track isn't even in the Olympics."

Dad never said anything like that again. He never pressured me. But he did believe in me. One person believing in you can give you great power, even if that one person is yourself.

I started thinking about the Olympics at age fifteen, after my first long-track race.

I competed in a pack race in Milwaukee, and friends talked me into staying to enter the Olympic speed skating trials.

"I don't know how to race against the clock," I told them. "You're out there in your own lane. I don't know what I'm doing."

They convinced me to take a risk and try.

I was the last one to skate, and the person I was paired with didn't show. So I skated alone. I worried I would forget to change lanes on the backstretch as required. I needed a time of 47 seconds and crossed the finish line in 46.7. I reacted as if I won a gold medal. One race and I qualified for the United States Olympic trials.

Frances M. Johnson

America's best skaters gathered two weeks later to
decide the U.S. Olympic team. The top five finishers from
my 500 event were chosen for the team. I finished eighth.

Coming close my first try made me want to work harder.

The national speed skating coaches started sending me
workout schedules. For the next three years I began training
more seriously.

Training by myself, away from coaches, proved difficult.
I skipped workouts sometimes during my high school days
to do things with my friends. I wasn't ready to have skating
be my whole life. I wanted to stay in school, be a
cheerleader and try other sports.

Frances M. Johnson

Summer–Fall

Monday: Rest

Tuesday: Slide board for
endurance, $1^1/_2$–2 hrs.

Wednesday: Weight training,
2–$2^1/_2$ hrs.; Bike ride for
endurance, $1^1/_2$ hrs.

Thursday: Bike work at interval
speeds, 2 hrs.

Friday: Slide board at interval
speeds, 2 hrs.; Intensive
endurance bike ride, 75 min.

Saturday: Weight training, 2–$2^1/_2$
hrs.; Endurance bike ride, 75
min.

Sunday: Interval running, $1^1/_2$ hrs.

Winter

Monday: Rest

Tuesday: Interval training on ice,
2 hrs. Weight training, 2 hrs.

Wednesday: Endurance ice
skating, $1^1/_2$ hrs.; Race
simulations, $1^1/_2$ hrs.

Thursday: Sprint skating, 2 hrs.;
Endurance bike ride, 1 hr.

Friday: Easy ice workout, 1 hr.;
Bike ride, 1 hr.

Saturday: Racing, 4 hrs. at rink;
Bike ride after, 30 min.

Sunday: Racing, 4 hrs. at rink:
Bike ride after, 75 min.

I soon realized to continue speed skating would take more dedication and more money for training. I didn't know what to do. I didn't want to use up all my parents' money on skating. I told a girlfriend, Tammy, about my problem while we were playing a softball game. She told her father, Jerry, who happened to work for the Champaign police department. He called me a few days later and said maybe he could help. We met for coffee one day and I explained needed about $7,000 a year to train. From that day, Jerry helped organize fund-raisers for me every year. My brother Rob and his friends started a golf tournament to raise money as well.

Sarajevo 1984

That money allowed me to train in Europe half the year and compete all over the world. It was rough sometimes, but every year all my needs were met. I never felt embarrassed using that money because sometimes we all need help from others. I was grateful to have such support.

As the 1984 Olympics approached, I felt ready. I made the team and went to Sarajevo, Yugoslavia, as it was called then. Just being in the opening ceremonies gave me goose bumps. Being around famous athletes in the cafeteria was almost as exciting as skating.

AP Photo

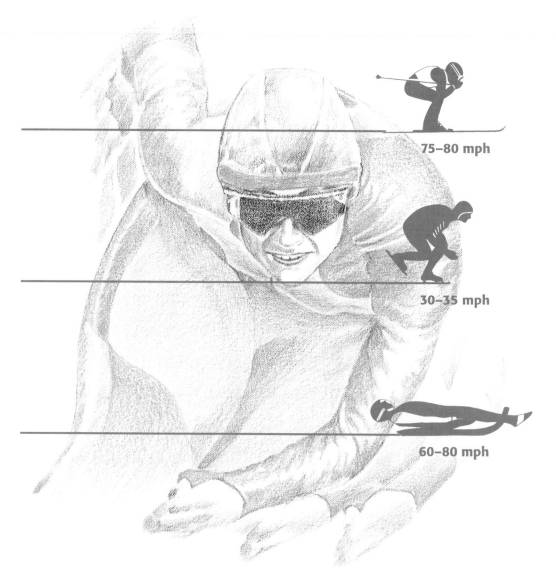

75–80 mph

30–35 mph

60–80 mph

Did you know the sport of speed skating is the fastest humans can go in the Olympics on their own power without the help of gravity? It's true. Speed skaters race on an oval ice track and glide around the track at speeds up to 30 miles per hour for women, 35 mph for men. In the Olympics, the skaters race two-by-two. The fastest time around the track wins. I did not have the best times in Sarajevo; I finished eighth in the 500. Even though I did not win a medal, I felt proud.

Focus on Sports

The next three years I trained longer and
~~har~~der and became a student of the sport,
~~lea~~rning as much as I could. My speed
~~inc~~reased, and my efforts started paying off in
~~19~~86 when I won a silver medal at the World
~~Sp~~rint championships. I earned a gold medal the
~~ne~~xt year in the same competition. Going into
~~the~~ 1988 Calgary Olympics, I knew I could
~~co~~mpete with the best in the world.

Dave Black

Calgary 1988

A group of about 25 traveled to Calgary, Canada, to support me. My family and friends became known as the Blair Bunch. The track in Calgary is one of the fastest in the world. The top skaters had their eye on breaking that 39-second barrier.

I always treated every race as if it were the Olympics, so when I raced in the Games I was mentally ready.

As I pushed toward the finish line in my 500 race, I knew I was on. I crossed the line and saw the clock flash 39.1, a new world record. I screamed in celebration.

Focus on Sports

Blair family

Moments before I stood on the victory stand, I saw my sisters, Suzy with a huge grin, Angela crying and Mary yelling. Rob was high-fiving people, and Mom had a scared-to-death look on her face. I felt all those emotions at once as I received my first Olympic gold medal.

Later, as I answered questions from the press, I spotted my dad in the room listening. I looked in his eyes and they glowed with pride. I'll never forget that look and bonding between us that night.

That night in Calgary proved to be the last big race my dad saw. His race was against the cancer in his body.

The next Christmas, the family gathered at Angela's house. We were playing family games on the night of December 23rd. Dad got up to go to bed at 10 o'clock, like always.

I remember him walking up the stairs. He stopped at the top and said, "Good night."

Then he gave a goodbye wave.

I had a nearby race the next morning. When none of my family showed up, I knew something was wrong. Dad went into a coma that day and died on Christmas night.

As you can imagine, that was a terribly sad time for our family. We all held up each other.

Death is a part of life, just as losing is a part of winning. Dad fought lung cancer for almost two years until it was his time.

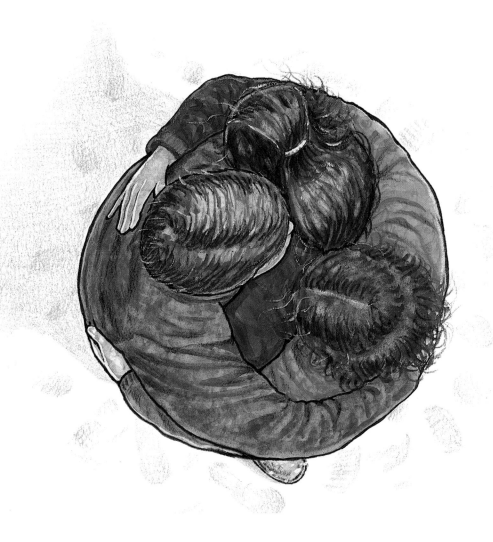

Our family had faced tough times before. We learned in 1986 that Rob had a tumor in his brain. Doctors said they could not operate, and Rob could die any minute or he could live a long time. The tumor causes horrible headaches and sometimes strikes him down with seizures, which makes him shake uncontrollably.

Rob has been positive and brave this whole time and battled his problem. He inspires me. Rob says his gold medal will be when he beats the tumor. Through helping each other and our faith, our family has survived our sadness.

Whenever there is tragedy, there also comes a time to move on. The clock of life keeps ticking. I couldn't bring Dad back, and I knew I had to skate forward. I went back to training, which often can be lonely. I've been lucky because I worked out with three of America's top skaters—Dan Jansen, a longtime family friend, Nick Thometz, who later became my coach, and Dave Cruikshank, my longtime boyfriend. Practicing with the best brought out the best in me. Skating with them made me faster. Three years flashed by and it was time for the next Olympics.

Bob Martin/Allsport USA

Albertville 1992

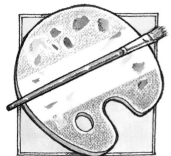

Because I won a gold medal in Calgary, people expected it would be easy for me to win again in Albertville. I never felt overconfident because no win in sports is guaranteed. I lost the World Cup Points Championship the year before when I fell in my last race.

Still, I never feared competition. Racing is why you train. I always figured after I paid the price in practice, the only thing left was to bring a positive attitude to the start line and do my best.

The Blair Bunch grew to 45 in France. They watched as I won gold medals in the 500 and 1,000 races. The victories were sweet, but the Games left a bitter taste for the U.S. team. For the second straight Olympics, Dan Jansen, the best skater in the world, went home without a medal.

Four years earlier, Dan's sister died of leukemia on the day of his first race in Calgary. He fell in both his races. In Albertville, Dan stayed on his skates, but finished fourth and twenty-sixth. Dan never acted jealous about my victories, and he congratulated me. I knew he hurt inside, though, and I wished I could share my medals with him.

A one-time change in the Winter Olympics schedule put the Games in Norway two years after Albertville. That gave Dan and me one last chance at the Olympics before we took off our racing skates for the last time.

Instead of resting on my victories and old ways, I changed coaches and my training habits. I took the risk because I had not clocked a personal best time in five years. I needed to try something different and make changes in my technique to improve.

Lillehammer 1994

The whole world hoped Dan would improve at the Lillehammer Games, his last chance at earning a medal. Dan's first race, in the 500, stunned everyone as he stumbled and failed to win a medal.

I watched the race at the Hamer rink and cried for my friend, knowing how hard Dan had worked. If anyone deserved a gold medal, he did.

Four days later, Dan lined up for his final race after being in four Olympics. I couldn't watch it in person. My first race was the next day, so I stayed at the athletes' village and watched it on TV.

My mom held her breath during my races and I found out why. I felt more nervous watching Dan than I did before I raced.

Worry quickly turned into joy as Dan won the 1,000 race in world record time. Tears streamed down my face as I jumped up and down in front of the TV while Dan took his victory lap. A few minutes later, I congratulated him thanks to a nearby official with a walkie-talkie.

I told him how proud I was of him. Even when Olympic fate had been unkind to him, Dan never lost his love for speed skating.

AP Photo/Thomas Kienzle

The Blair Bunch overflowed with 60 people when my turn to race came. I never felt added pressure with my family and friends there. That's because I knew they would love me no matter what happened.

Fortunately we were able to celebrate two more times as I finished first in the 500 and 1,000. After the 500 win, I climbed up into the stands to be with the Bunch and thank them for all their support.

Jerry Lampen/Reut

I also raced in the longer 1,500-meter event. Being a
printer, the longer races were not my strength. I decided to
try anyway.

I finished three-one-hundredths of a second behind the
third-place skater, which meant I missed a bronze medal by
the time it takes to snap your fingers.

Sure I would have treasured another medal, but I was not
disappointed. I skated my fastest time ever in the event.

After the Olympics, I had offers to come home and cash in on my medals with TV commercials. I stayed in Europe to compete and train for my race against the clock. That decision paid off a month later in Calgary.

On the same track where Dad saw me win my first gold medal, I returned to try for the 39-second barrier with only a few hundred people watching.

My start was perfect, and I felt a slingshot push in the backstretch. Rounding the final corner, I saw the clock and knew this was my chance. I put my head down and gave it my all. I crossed the line and looked up to see: 38.99, a new world record. Eleven months later, I broke my own record again at 38.69.

Topping my personal best proved just as satisfying as winning a gold medal.

Few people compete in the Olympics, but everyone can better themselves.

You can too by finding something you love to do and dedicating yourself to it. Be willing to risk your pride and remember to keep a balance in your life, with the help of faith, friends and family. When you do these things, you will have a winning edge.